In the Shadows of the Garden

Also by Sharon Kernot and published by Ginninderra Press
Washday Pockets

Sharon Kernot

In the Shadows
of the Garden

Acknowledgements

'A Family Christmas' was first published in 2003 by Wakefield Press in *Cracker! A Christmas Collection*. 'In the Shadows of the Garden' was published in *Pendulum* 2005. 'Murder in Underground Road' was first published by Queensland University of Technology in *Idiom* 23. 'Imagine' was presented in 2006 at Mawson Lakes as the opening address at a conference entitled Working with Disadvantage: We Can't Do It Alone. 'In Our Street' was published in 2008 in the Federation of Australian Writers (Vic) anthology entitled *The Envelope Please* and 'Standing Tall' was published in 2009 in the Federation of Australia Writers (Vic) anthology of winning entries from their 2008 literary awards.

GINNINDERRA PRESS
PO Box 3461 Port Adelaide SA 5015
www.ginninderrapress.com.au

Contents

In the Shadows of the Garden

'What the hell is this?' Dad's voice booms through the thin-walled house.

Peter smiles at me and shrugs. He's the oldest.

'Look! There's a trail of it,' Mum says. I imagine her pointing at something. Something of mine maybe. But what?

I look at Peter. The corners of his mouth are turned up in a little smirk. His eyebrows leap and his eyes sparkle back at me as if he's read my thoughts. He's never caught, he's too careful. Mum thinks he's an angel. Ha! If only she knew. I call him Perfect Peter.

'Where'd it go?'

Mum and Dad are close now, just down the hall.

'Look! There it is.'

'What is it?'

'Something sticky.'

I glance at Stevie. His bottom lip is trembling; a piece of Lego drops from his hand.

'Look there's a pool of it here,' Mum says. 'In here with the kids.'

None of us move. Peter's smirk disappears.

Dad dives to the floor, crawls around on hands and knees and looks under the bed. He drags out Stevie's school bag and glances inside. 'Found it!' He opens the bag for Mum to see.

She leans forward, peers into the damp, darkness and reels back in disgust. 'Oh, my God!'

'What the hell is this?' Dad roars at Stevie and waves the bag wildly.

Droplets fly around the room. One cool, clear drop lands on my hand. Its fragrance is familiar. Mum grabs the bag and carries it carefully, at arm's length, out of the room.

Dad stands over Stevie and roars, 'Get outside. Now!' He points at the door with one hand and gives him a slap with the other. 'Come on, all of you, up and out.' He never misses an opportunity to lecture us together.

Outside on the safety of the grass, Dad tips the contents of the bag onto the lawn. His face is set in a scowl; his eyebrows join in one thick, black line.

The bag spews out slimy, juice-drenched plastic wrap, a slippery pencil, a soggy exercise book, six mouldy Vegemite sandwiches and one slimy slice of watermelon peel. Dad stands with his hands on his hips and looks down at the mouldy, sticky mass. I hear the back door creak and thud shut as Mum retreats into the house.

Dad's long thick eyebrow casts a dark shadow over his face. He turns to Stevie and glares. 'Watermelon.' He shakes his head and begins his lecture. 'Who gave you permission to take watermelon to school?'

There's no need to reply.

Stevie is small for his age and thin, very thin. His head is round like a melon and large. On his skinny frame and with his sticky-out ears, it looks enormous.

'What gives you the right…' Dad continues.

Stevie's huge head hangs as he stares at the mouldy mass. A tear clings to the end of his nose.

It was only yesterday that we had tasted the sweet melon. A rare treat. We sat circular on the grass as if we were having a secret powwow and we ate the cool slices in the shadows of the garden. Our tepee, made of two ragged sheets and a broken broom handle, sat under the shade of the nectarine tree.

Peter had stolen one of Mum's Marlboro Gold cigarettes and had it tucked behind his ear. He snatched it out and held it up. 'First we feast, then we smoke peace pipe,' he said.

I checked my watermelon wedge carefully for black seeds. They looked like beetles in the pink flesh. I flicked them out as I saw them and cleared the way so I could have a good, clean bite.

Peter ate his melon savagely, one large chunk after another. Never mind the seeds, the ammunition. Whenever his tongue found a seed he aimed and spat it. One hit my arm. Another, my eye.

'Stop it!' I warned.

'I'm trying to get it in your ear, Jenny,' he said, as if that made it all right. He aimed and a seed whizzed passed my nose.

'Cut it out!' I thumped his arm hard, as hard as I could.

'Didn't hurt.' He laughed and punched me with an iron fist.

I blinked back tears and rubbed my arm.

'Cry baby, cry baby.' He spat another seed. It bounced off my cheek.

I clenched my fist and my teeth and glared at him.

'Hey, look at this,' Stevie said.

I ignored him.

Peter pretended to ignore me.

'Look!' Stevie called.

I wouldn't look. I knew what he was doing. I kept glaring at Peter, who was laughing and pointing at Stevie.

'Look!' Stevie danced like a lunatic between us with the watermelon peel over his mouth in the shape of a giant smile. He looked ridiculous. A giant head with a giant smile and a tiny, stick insect body.

I didn't want to laugh, to be won over, like when Dad tickled us and made us giggle when really we wanted to cry.

Stevie kept on. He turned the smile upside-down and danced a depressed dance with drooping shoulders. He turned his smiley peel again and again. Happy. Sad. Happy. Sad. Then he snatched the Marlboro from behind Peter's ear and pretended to smoke it, first himself and then with the watermelon grin.

'Peace,' he roared again and again until I couldn't hold back the laughter any more.

No one is laughing now as Dad bellows over us. 'Waste, waste, bloody waste.… Look at all those mouldy sandwiches.'

We stare down at the mass of slimy, mouldy Vegemite sand-wiches.

'And the watermelon. Look at that. Crushed. Wasted. Bloody mush.' He shakes his head slowly. 'Watermelon does not travel well.'

I wonder how a watermelon might travel well. In a car? A bus maybe? I could see it would not be comfortable in Stevie's school bag because he likes to play football with it.

'If I ever, ever, bloody ever, find another mouldy sandwich in your bag. Or mushed-up melon…' Dad pauses for effect, as always, making sure he has our full attention before delivering the punchline. 'I'll make you eat them.' He pauses again. 'Is that clear?'

'Yes,' we all murmur and continue to look down at the slushy mess.

I sneak a sideways glance at Stevie; he has a greenish tinge. Peter's smirk is back but it's well hidden behind his long fringe.

'Now clean it up!' Dad marches into the house giving the back door a hard slam on the way through.

'What were you thinking?' Peter asks.

Stevie shrugs and wipes the tears from his cheeks.

'You have to be more careful. You have to hide the evidence. If you don't eat your sandwich, you throw it in the bin at school. Don't you, Jenny?'

'That's right,' I say. 'Or you chuck it under the house like Peter does.'

Peter bends down and rearranges the contents of the bag into the shape of a face: eyes, nose, hair, eyebrow and mouth. Stevie tips his head and stares at the shape for a moment. Suddenly his eyes gleam with recognition, his body begins to shake and he falls to the ground. Peter and I collapse beside him. The three of us hoot and laugh and roll around on the grass and the watermelon grins between us.

The Community Centre

Warm winter sun streams in through the lace curtains in the lounge and Mary reminds herself she has much to be grateful for. She glances at the clock on the dresser. It's almost ten. Jack will be home from his morning walk soon and will want to head off to do the grocery shopping. She sighs. She hates shopping with Jack.

He has to check the value of every item he puts into the trolley. It's difficult to mask her annoyance and frustration as they traipse from aisle to aisle. Everything has to be measured according to cost and this can be difficult because as Jack points out, you have to compare apples with apples. So Jack reduces the cost of each item down to its base unit – the price per gram or kilo, litre or millilitre – so he can compare. It's so time-consuming and tedious that Mary sighs again at the task ahead. She's due at the community centre at twelve to help out with the free lunches. She'd prefer to get there earlier but that won't be possible with the shopping on the agenda first.

The cuckoo clock in the entrance hall creaks and the wooden doors open. The tiny bird pops out and begins to cuckoo the hour. Jack will be back any second. She leans forward, cranes her neck in the direction of the park and there he is walking briskly with Rex, their golden retriever, at his side. Mary fastens the top button of her woollen, navy cardigan, smooths her plaid skirt and reaches for her handbag so she will be ready to leave the minute Jack is organised. Out in the street, there is a sudden shout and savage barking. She rushes to the window. A tall, grey-haired man blocks the gate so Jack can't pass. Rex growls and snaps the air and Jack tries to hold him back.

'Let me through,' Jack shouts at the man.

Mary opens the front door and dithers, uncertain of what to do.

Is the man a real threat? She's seen him trudging up and down many times but he seemed harmless.

'Here is your prison cell, your prison smell, your smelling, stinking, smouldering onion cage.' He rattles the gate and bangs a fist on the top of the letterbox.

Rex snarls.

'Let me pass!'

'Smelling, stinking, rotting jail cell smell...' He pounds his chest with his fist.

Mary's heart thumps. 'Jack?' she calls. 'Shall I call the police?'

'Yes! Call the police!'

She scurries down the passage to the kitchen, snatches the cordless phone from the cradle and dials triple zero as she races back to the front door. When she gets there, Jack is standing inside the gate watching the crazed man stride down the street calling profanities to the air, his arms striking at invisible demons.

Mary turns the phone off. 'Are you all right?' she asks Jack as he comes through the door.

'I'm fine,' he says brushing white dog hairs from his black trousers. 'Fine.' But she can see he isn't. His hands are shaking and there's a shimmer of sweat on his brow.

***

Mary takes the large frypan off the stove and places it into the steaming, lemon-scented water to soak while she heads out to the dining room to see how things are going. The community centre is getting busy already and it's only just turned twelve. The stench of unwashed bodies and wet, sweat-filled shoes fill the passage. It's a smell Mary imagines she will never get used to and something she has struggled with since she began working for the community centre a year ago.

She reminds herself to be kind. She is privileged. She had a solid working-class upbringing where cleanliness was of the utmost importance. She, like her own mother, prides herself on her clean home, her sparkling windows, her white whites and her well-pressed clothes. Jack is the same. The garden and shed are immaculate. The gutters are cleaned regularly, the lawn is edged and mowed, the hedges are trimmed and the car is polished. Nothing is out of place.

An uneasiness that Mary struggles to decipher nudges her but vanishes the instant she passes a pungent old man in the double doorway. Once inside the dining room, the reek of unwashed bodies mixes with the smell of two varieties of soup. Mary stands near the fragrant pots to relieve her nostrils. The room is noisy with the deep rumble of men's voices. She clutches her apron, surveys the room and wonders if there will be enough seats and enough food. The cold weather brings the homeless and needy in from far and wide and even though the day was looking cheerful this morning, it has taken a turn. The sky has darkened and the rain looks as if it will begin early.

'There's a storm coming,' a man wearing a bright orange jacket calls as if reading Mary's thoughts. Though she's not sure he is talking about the weather and he certainly isn't speaking to her. She has learnt, since working for the Centre that many of the people who come are mentally unstable, many incapable of looking after themselves properly. Most live a transient life – lonely and chaotic.

Mary turns to watch Jan and Erica ladle soup into an assortment of chipped ceramic bowls. She and another volunteer, Maureen, will serve. She takes a large box of buttered bread rolls and a pair of tongs, and begins to move up and down the trestle tables. She puts a roll on the small plate next to each place and watches as grimy, nicotine-stained fingers snatch them up. She works quickly. There are many rolls and the men will eat more than one each. Some will eat until there is no food left.

Once she has placed a roll next to each man, she goes back to collect two bowls of soup – one of each variety. Although there are two choices, most of the men will take whatever she has in her hand because they are so hungry.

She walks to the end of the table. 'Minestrone?'

'Thank you.' A young man with dark circles around his eyes reaches out to take the bowl but she expertly avoids his grasp and places the soup neatly in front of him.

The room becomes progressively quieter as more men eat. Mary walks swiftly back and forth until everyone has a bowl of soup and then she goes back to the kitchen.

She takes a scrubbing brush from the cupboard under the sink and begins to work on the soaking frypan. She thinks back to the morning's events – the madman and the shopping. She wonders if Jack has called the police as he said he would. He was still very agitated at the shops, his hands continued to shake and he couldn't concentrate on the calculations. Instead they bought the brands they most often buy and the shopping took half the time. Mary managed to get to the Centre early to help prepare lunch and the shopping cost about the same as it always did.

'Mary?' Lucia, the coordinator of the Centre, touches her on the arm and Mary jumps.

'You caught me in a daydream.' Mary says. She turns and is stunned to see the tall gangly man that harassed Jack that morning standing next to Lucia.

'This is Kenneth,' Lucia says.

The man nods a greeting at Mary. His hands are gathered into huge knots at his side.

'Will you take Kenneth to the dining room for soup?'

Mary stares at Kenneth, who stares blankly back. The incident ricochets around inside her head. She doesn't know what to say. Doesn't know what to do. She considers telling Lucia that she's too busy. That she has to finish an urgent job for someone. She has to finish scrubbing the pan. Obviously she can't mention what happened this morning, not now, not with him standing so close.

'Everything okay?' Lucia raises her dark eyebrows in concern.

Mary looks into Kenneth's face but sees nothing to fear. His eyes are placid, his limbs quiet – he doesn't seem to recognise her at all. She relaxes a little. Decides to take him to the dining room and speak to Lucia about it when she returns. 'Yes,' she says. 'Of course. Yes.' She dries her hands briskly on her apron. 'Come this way, Kenneth.'

She braces herself as he follows her down the long passage toward the dining room. She must be mad. He could hit her. Would he? She turns but there is still no sign of malice in his face. It is calm – almost gentle. Is it possible that he just had a troubled morning? Perhaps taken his medication a little late? He certainly seems stable now. Mary doesn't know very much about mental illness but there are a few schizophrenics who attend the Centre and she's noticed that they are well most of the time. She opens a door to the hall and motions for Kenneth to enter. He flashes her a gappy brown-toothed grin that she finds strangely reassuring.

They walk to the serving table and Mary takes a small white plate, places a large crusty roll on it and hands it to Kenneth.

'Thank you, ma'am.' He holds the plate out awkwardly in front of him.

'We have two types of soup today – minestrone or chicken and vegetable.'

Kenneth smiles and nods. 'Thank you, ma'am.'

Such good manners. There's no sign of the morning madness. Not even a hint. 'Which one would you like to start with?'

'Min-e-strohh-nee,' he articulates in an overly dramatic Italian accent that makes Mary smile.

She takes a bowl and fills it with soup. 'I'll carry this for you,' she says. 'Let's go and find somewhere to sit.' She glances around the room in search of a place that isn't too cramped. She has seen Kenneth's arms thrash about and she doesn't want any accidents or fights to break out.

'Here we are.' She places the bowl of soup down and pulls out a plastic chair for him.

'Thank you, ma'am.' Kenneth bows flamboyantly and flashes his imperfect smile. 'You are wonn-derr-ous.'

Wonderous? The word is sung in a resonant baritone.

'Grreeeetings,' he sings to the men around him. They nod back.

Mary giggles and shakes her head at the change in the man. He's such a character and so…likeable. Is this the same person who was shouting abuse at her husband this morning? Perhaps Jack was merely in the wrong place at the wrong time. Surely it was nothing personal. She hopes he doesn't phone the police after all. She feels a pang of guilt and a vague sense of disloyalty for Jack at the unexpected warmth she feels for the wild man. She leaves Kenneth with his soup and walks back to the kitchen feeling uneasy, feeling perplexed and concerned by her conflicting emotions.

She takes up the scrubbing brush and begins to work on the frypan again. She thinks about the morning's events – the incident with Kenneth and Jack. Her uneasiness swirls around inside her like the grey bubbles in the tepid dishwater. She works hard on the pan and eventually manages to shift all the grease and grime. As she dries it off with a tea towel, she decides not to judge herself so harshly about her conflicting feelings. Perhaps, like the shopping, there is no need to dissect the value of every item and no need to divide life into tiny units of right and wrong.

Killing Him Softly

The memory of the children leaving, the calling of 'Bye, Mum' and the door slamming replay over and over in Louise's head.

'Jeez, Louise, I wish I had every second weekend to myself,' her best friend, Karen, often said.

'You'd soon change your mind.'

'Not a cat's chance,' she'd say. 'No way.'

Louise doubted it. She'd been in the same situation. She'd often wished her husband (ex-husband) John, would take the kids out for a couple of hours or come home early and spend time with them while she cooked dinner. But he never did and when he finally sauntered through the door with his suit jacket slung over his shoulder in that sexy way, she always forgave him. She'd forgive him for anything. Back then she would have given anything to have a day off to go shopping but now she has every moment of every second weekend to herself, she can't enjoy it.

As the echo of the door fades and the silence closes in, she wonders what to do with the long stretch of time before her. Her friends have suggested she join an on-line dating site. Louise shudders at the thought. Secretly, she hopes John and his new partner, Wendy, have an almighty row and John returns home with his jacket slung over his shoulder and a sheepish grin on his face.

She knows it's unlikely. As time moves along, it seems clear John and Wendy are likely to play Happy House forever. Even the children adore Wendy.

The phone rings and startles Louise from her daydream. She sits on the edge of her chair and listens as the answering machine clicks in.

'Louise? It's me – Karen. Pick up.'

Louise doesn't move. She doesn't feel like talking to anyone, not even to Karen.

'I'm waiting,' Karen says.

Louise holds her breath and sits very still as if trying to camouflage herself from a predator.

'Louise!' Karen barks. 'Come on, pick up. I know you're there. You're always there.'

'Ugh!' Louise snatches up the phone. 'Hello.'

'I knew you were there, you bugger!' Karen snorts gleefully. 'How's it going?'

'Okay…the kids have just left.'

'Good.'

'Good?'

'Good – it's your weekend off. I'm having a few people round tonight.'

'Ahh…no… I'd rather –'

'Don't be stupid. Adult company is just what you need to get yourself out of the doldrums.'

Adult company is exactly what Louise was trying to avoid.

'Distractions, that's what you need,' Karen says. 'So you can dig yourself out of the morbid little hole you're in.'

Louise sighs.

'It's just a casual barbecue with a few friends from work. You'll like them, they're fun. It starts at seven.'

'I dunno. I really don't feel like –'

'Come on. It'll do you good.'

Louise doesn't say anything.

'There's a very nice single man coming.'

'No!' Louise reels at the thought – a man.

'His name's Tom.'

'No.'

'You'll like him,' she croons. 'He's a bit of a hottie.'

The word 'hottie' sends a shock wave of panic through Louise. 'No way. Absolutely not.'

'What the hell… Why not?'

'Just no,' Louise says firmly.

Karen tuts. 'Well, you know where we are. You know the time. If you manage to come to your senses and crawl out of your morbid cesspit by then, make sure you wear something gorgeous.' She hangs up.

Louise wishes her friends would leave her alone, wishes they would let her heal at her own pace. Karen disagrees. She says she won't heal until she takes off her rose-coloured glasses.

Louise wanders into the kitchen, opens the pantry and stares at her condiments lined up as neatly as tin soldiers. Every melamine shelf, every can and jar shines and sparkles bleakly back. She shuts the door and opens the fridge. It too gleams with an unnatural cleanliness. Over the months, Louise has scrubbed and tidied everything. The lonely evenings when the children are in bed are just as bad as the weekends. She misses those long conversations with John about his work. For a long time, she supposes, she lived vicariously through his work adventures. At least she had while the children were very young and before she'd started working part-time.

She wanders into Daniel and Jake's room and begins to strip the sheets from their beds. She loved that part-time job. She wishes she'd taken it on full-time when it was offered. It was much more satisfying than her current job. She bundles the sheets into a tight ball and heads to the laundry. A knot of annoyance at the thought of the lost job opportunity swells in the pit of her stomach. She pushes it aside. If she had known then what she knows now, she would have taken the job. But she wasn't to know. How could she?

'Bollocks!' Karen's voice shouts in her head. 'Take a good hard look at yourself. Take a good hard look at him. Jeez, Louise, you are the Denial Queen.'

Louise prefers to think of herself as optimistic. She drops the sheets and pillowcases onto the cold laundry tiles and opens the lid of the gleaming washing machine. The lost job does annoy her though, no use pretending otherwise. Her current job – selling retro clothing to middle-class women – isn't so great. In fact, it's mind-blowingly boring on a quiet day. The other one was interesting, challenging. But two days a week didn't even cover the mortgage repayments so when John left she had to give it up and find a full-time job after all.

She dumps a cup of lemon-scented washing powder into the machine, presses the 'ON' button, picks up the sheets from the floor and loads them carefully, distributes them evenly so they will not unbalance the machine during the spin cycle. She shuts the lid and stares at the dials, stares at the red setting. Hot. Hottie. God! What on earth would she talk about? What on earth was Karen thinking?

She leaves the thought behind in the laundry and wanders into Sophie's room. Sporty Barbie, Wedding Barbie and Groomsman Ken are scattered about the floor along with a pile of tiny Barbie trinkets – wine glasses, silver and gold shoes, tiny knives, forks and spoons, and a wedding cake. Sophie loves Barbie as much as Louise had when she was a girl.

She kneels down onto the pale grey carpet to tidy up, relieved her daughter has left the room untidy. Relieved she has found something to occupy her time. She smooths Wedding Barbie's hair and seats her at the dining table in the Barbie house. She sits Ken opposite and places a wineglass in front of each of them. Ken looks handsome in his suit, bow tie and dark, neatly clipped hair. A little like John – a lot like John.

'He's quite a catch,' Louise says to Wedding Barbie. 'Lucky you.' She places the three-tiered wedding cake between them and sets the small table as if they are about to be served dinner.

Wedding Barbie looks stunning in her white, satin dress. Louise has always thought of herself as Wedding Barbie but as she glances at Sporty Barbie, sprawled on the floor beside the house, she realises this is now her reality. Wedding Barbie is actually Wendy.

Will John and Wendy marry? She picks up Sporty Barbie and smooths her ponytail, lifts her sunglasses and dabs at invisible tears.

'It'll be okay,' she says. 'It'll work out.' She looks at Ken and Wedding Barbie sitting happily at the table and wishes it were her and John. A memory and the words La-la Land leap into her head.

It was about three years ago when Louise had been offered that full-time job. She was thrilled. John wasn't happy. He wasn't interested in her working full-time. The house only needed one breadwinner, he said. And that was him.

'But it could use two,' she'd argued. 'And then maybe you won't need to work so late all the time. We might even see more of each other.' She'd imagined them spending long evenings chatting about their working days over a glass of red wine while the children were in bed. 'Why can't we share the workload? Have two breadwinners?'

'I'm not giving up my job, my career, just so you can play feminazi!'

'Feminazi?' She felt as if she'd been slapped. It was a term he had used before to describe monstrous, aggressive women at work – or so she thought. She was horrified he'd used it to describe her. She was a good wife, a good mother. She backed down. She didn't want to upset the balance.

'Feminazi? You? Ha!' Karen's reaction was just as insulting. 'You're more like a Stepford Wife.'

'Well, thank you very much.'

'I'm the feminazi,' Karen said, goose-stepping around the family room. 'I'll give him feminazi, the arrogant –'

'He's not that bad. He's just old-fashioned.' Louise felt a pang of guilt for discussing him negatively. 'He's a good husband, a good provider.'

'La-la Land, that's where you live. Those rose-coloured glasses of yours have got to go. He's manipulative.'

'What?'

'He's just playing with that need-to-please personality of yours to get whatever he wants.'

Was he? Possibly. Even so, Louise decides not to be too hard on herself. Surely it's commendable to try to do the right thing, to try and keep a marriage together despite its problems. And there were, she supposes, a few of those. It wasn't just the fact that he wasn't home much and didn't spend much time with her and the children. It was the lies.

She narrows her eyes at Ken and waggles her finger in his face. 'The beer on your breath, the lipstick on your collar that time and those midnight texts.' Louise takes a deep stabbing breath. She should have said something. Anything.

Well, at least the children had a stable home for many years. She didn't have to work unless she wanted to, didn't have to put them into day care in the early days. She loved being at home for them. That was the good thing about working part-time. She was always there. Always…except once. She glares at Ken. He looks back benignly just as John had then. The angry knot in her stomach tightens as another memory comes into focus.

Louise had to go to a compulsory office planning day over the other side of town and wasn't able to pick the children up from school. The boys happened to be on camp at the time so it was only Sophie she had to worry about. She arranged for her to go into after school care and asked John to pick her up before it closed at six o'clock.

The planning day went well. Louise enjoyed it. She drove off feeling invigorated and motivated. When she turned her mobile phone on to check her messages, there was one from the school.

'It is now six p.m. and no one has arrived to collect Sophie. Please call back immediately. The centre has closed.'

Louise was mortified.

There was a second message. And a third.

She looked at her watch. It was half past six! She phoned the school with her heart in her throat.

A woman answered after one ring. 'SunnyValeAfter-SchoolHours.'

'Hello, it's Sophie's mum, Louise. I've just–'

'How far away are you? I've got to get home. I've got my own children, you know.'

'I'm sorry. Is Sophie still there?'

'Yes.'

'Oh God! Is she all right?' Louise couldn't hide the panic in her voice. 'My husband was supposed to pick her up.'

'I've tried his number. There's no reply.'

'I'll phone–'

'When can you get here?'

'I'm on the other side of town. The traffic's heavy. It'll take an hour, maybe more…'

The woman sighs loudly.

'I'll try John and call you straight back.' Louise hung up and fumbled with her phone, found Darling John in the contact list and selected 'call'. It went straight to his message bank. She tried his office number just in case he was still at work but there was no answer there. She tried his mobile again and again without response. Something must have happened.

She dialled Karen's number.

'Hi, you've reached Kaz and Co. Sorry we're busy. Leave…'

Louise went through her list. She tried family and friends but no one answered. In between each she tried John's number. Where the hell was he? Surely he wouldn't just leave little Sophie at after school care unless something awful had happened. She wondered if he'd had a car accident or a heart attack.

Her phone rang – it was the centre.

'Hello?' she said breathlessly, hopefully. Maybe John had arrived or phoned to say he was on his way.

'How's it going?' The impatient voice asked. 'It's getting later and later.'

'I'm still trying. I'm sorry… I have no idea where John is.'

'You do realise we charge a dollar per minute once the centre closes.'

'Yes, of course. How's Sophie? Is she okay?'

'She's okay. She's drawing a picture – a family portrait.'

'The poor little thing.'

'Indeed.'

'Something must have happened…'

Louise's phone began to bleep in her ear.

'I have a call. It might be John.' She hung up and looked at the caller ID – it was him. 'John!' she gasped.

'Yep. You've been trying to call?'

The calmness in his voice was so contrary to her own feelings she felt wounded.

'You there? What's up?'

'What's up? I thought you were dead!'

'What? What do you mean, dead?'

'You were supposed to pick up Sophie.'

'Ah. Oh yeah.'

'She's still there. So I thought you must have been in some terrible, life-threatening accident. I thought you must have been dead or at the very least bleeding to death.'

'Don't be so melodramatic. I was called into a meeting. An important meeting. I got held up that's all. I just forgot about her.'

'Forgot?'

'Can't you get her? I'm still twenty maybe thirty minutes away.'

Louise gripped the steering wheel and watched her knuckles turn white. 'I'm over the other side of town,' she said slowly through her teeth. 'We agreed you would do it. Just this once. I can't believe you forgot her.'

'I told you it was an important meeting.'

'I don't care! Just get there as soon as you can.'

'All right, all right, keep your hair on.'

She hung up. She couldn't listen any more. She felt like throwing the phone through the front window. She wanted to stomp on it. Stomp on him.

She called the school back and apologised. She explained that her very busy, very important husband had clean forgotten.

'I'd kill him,' the other woman said. 'If my husband did that, I'd kill him.'

'Yes.' Louise nodded. Right then she could have. But instead she buried the memory. Conveniently. Those old rose-coloured glasses worked their magic as always.

Louise gazes at the dolls in Barbie Land. At Ken sitting smugly with Wendy enjoying his life while she stays home grieving.

'Pathetically wallowing in self-pity,' Karen's voice corrects.

Pushed aside to rot like Sporty Barbie. Louise snatches Ken from his seat and undresses him then sits his naked, plastic body back down again opposite Wedding Barbie.

'There he is,' she says. She takes off Sporty Barbie's sunglasses and tosses them aside. 'Now we see him fully, don't we?'

Sporty Barbie nods in agreement.

'Take a good hard look, Wedding Barbie, Wedding Wendy. You sound like a nice lady. Don't let him push you around.'

Wedding Barbie doesn't comment and Louise supposes she will find out in her own good time if they are meant to live happily ever after or at least ever after.

Louise puts away the rest of the tiny Barbie trinkets and stands Sporty Barbie on top of Sophie's tallboy.

The soothing sound of balanced sheets spinning in the washing machine rumbles around the house as Louise enters her bedroom. She strips the cool sheets from her bed, leaves them in a pile by the door and opens her wardrobe to see if it needs a clean out. It does. For some unknown reason she has kept her maternity clothes, her post-pregnancy pants and a whole pile of drab, ill-fitting tops and skirts that don't suit her any more. Did they ever? She pulls them out, folds them and places them neatly into canvas bags to take to the shop on Monday.

When she's finished, the wardrobe looks bare, uncomfortably stark. She checks her watch and decides to go shopping. She has plenty of time to kill and some new clothes might brighten her up, make her feel better. And, if she happens to find something 'gorgeous' while she's out, she might, just might, decide to go to Karen's barbecue after all.

A Family Christmas

'I don't want to sit next to Uncle Billy again.'

'Oh, really, Janet. He's not that bad.'

'Yes, he is. He doesn't wash from one Christmas to the next.'

'You are sitting here. Uncle Billy is there.' Betty positioned the name cards at the beautifully set table.

'Not opposite! No.' Janet folded her arms and shook her head. She knew she sounded like a child; Betty always brought that out in her. 'I'll have to watch all the food spill out of his mouth when he talks.'

'Shush! He'll hear you.' Betty put a plump finger to coral pink lips then folded her arms and pursed her mouth. The matter was closed.

Janet pouted and stomped out of the room, slamming the screen door as she went outside. She was angry with herself. Why, at thirty-eight years of age, did she have so much trouble standing up to her mother? Why did she always regress to her old child self? Did other women have the same problem? She wondered if her relationship with her mother would ever evolve beyond this point.

She wandered outside to watch her own children, Natalie and Jack, playing in the garden. She was much softer with them and encouraged them to be assertive. They were leaning over the small fishpond talking in whispers when she walked up behind them.

'What are you two up to?'

'Nothing,' they said in unison.

Janet sighed. This was her children's favourite word. They both used it repeatedly. That and 'good'. Every day was the same.

'How was school?'

'Good.'

'What did you do?'

'Nothing.'

How did other families communicate? Funny how she had taken a completely different approach to child-rearing from her mother and yet they had landed in the same place, in the same hole.

'Better get in,' she told them. 'Granddad will want to sort the presents.'

Jack and Natalie ran inside squealing. Janet heard her mother shush them. She folded her arms and looked down into the fishpond at a goldfish skimming for food. She noticed her reflection wavering on the surface. From this angle, she could be her mother.

She walked inside just in time to see Betty greeting Wayne at the door. Wayne bent down to hug his mother and she kissed him affectionately on the cheek. He rose with a large coral-pink smudge on his face. Or was he just glowing? Who was that girl with him? Very attractive, blonde hair, slim figure and half his age. Ugh! Look at him wearing leather pants and a trendy shirt left hanging out, probably to hide his large middle-aged paunch. They came in holding hands.

Janet put on her smile. 'Hello, Wayne.' If she had turned up with a man half her age, her mother would have had a fit. There wouldn't be any coral kisses for her.

Wayne introduced them. 'Kylie, this is my sister Janet.'

Kylie smiled sweetly. She stepped forward and held out a hand the colour and texture of white satin. A child's hand. Why couldn't he settle for a medallion or a motorbike?

Janet took the satin fingers gently; they were warm and damp. She couldn't be more than nineteen. 'You're just in time for the opening ceremony.'

'Sorry?'

'We're about to open the presents.'

Kylie followed Janet into the lounge, where the children sat squirming, waiting to be handed their presents. This ritual had gone on for as long as Janet could remember. Except now it was her own children who sat at the base of the tree sorting through presents, shaking them and trying to guess what they were.

'What a beautiful tree,' Kylie said.

The Christmas tree was over six feet tall. It was decorated with expensive trinkets, some of which had been in the family since Janet was a girl, others had been bought from countries around the world. Gold and silver tinsel were wound with meticulous precision around the tree. Coloured fairy lights flashed day and night for the full Christmas season.

'Put some music on, George,' Betty told Janet's father.

He shuffled around for a moment and then Bing Crosby's *I'm Dreaming of a White Christmas* crooned from the speakers.

Janet sat down on the olive-green sofa and waited for her father to get started. The air conditioner cooled the odorous air. The room had changed little in thirty-eight Christmases. The same velvet lounge suite and leather recliners, beige carpet, the ornately framed Constable prints and the dozen or so photographs of the family. Even the satin-finish wallpaper with subtle pinstripe remained. Only the wedding photos of Wayne and his ex-wife had been removed and the remaining photos reshuffled to fill the gaps.

Uncle Billy sat wheezing mildly in the armchair opposite. 'Come on,' he told George. 'Let's get moving so we can eat.'

George held a present out at arm's length trying to read the label. He ran a thick, sun-tanned hand through his thin grey hair.

'That's for our little fellow Jack,' Betty told him. 'Where are your glasses?'

He shrugged and passed the present to Jack, who was eagerly waiting.

'Here, have mine.' Betty passed him her reading glasses.

Janet sneaked a glance at Kylie, who was watching George with interest as he read the labels of the Christmas tags in Betty's pink-framed specs. She sat close to Wayne with her arm looped through his, holding a big square hand between both of hers.

Janet looked over at her husband, John. When was the last time they held hands? He was holding a can of Carlton Draught and already well on his way to anaesthetising himself. He wore his oldest pair of shorts, his legs were spread apart and from this angle, she could see his red jocks. At least they looked Christmassy. He scratched at the grey stubble on his chin. He hadn't even shaved.

George sifted through the presents. He always tried to be fair, to find something for each person rather than have people sit with nothing. When the children had a gift each, he gave one to each adult, even Kylie. Who was it from, Wayne or Betty? Janet realised that her mother must have known about Kylie for some time and hadn't told her. In fact, her mother seemed to be quite comfortable with this new addition to the clan and not at all upset about the departure of the other. The discarded wife and daughter-in-law of twenty years. It seemed odd that someone had stepped so quickly and easily into another's place.

She looked at Wayne, smiling and animated, then to John as he took another mouthful of beer. Was there a midlife crisis pending beneath that stubble and glazed stare? How would John's parents react if he separated and came home with another woman? Would she be so easily forgotten?

Janet watched Kylie tear the wrapping paper off the present with all the excitement of a child. Inside, there was a very small but expensive bottle of Angel perfume.

'My favourite!' She gave Betty and then George an enthusiastic hug and kiss on the cheek. 'Thank you!'

George flushed, adjusted his glasses, cleared his throat and went back to his job.

The children were getting restless. 'What else have we got, Granddad?'

George ignored them and carried on in his methodical way: one for Uncle Billy, one for Janet…

'Granddad?'

One for John, one for Wayne…

'What's there for me, Granddad?'

'Shush. Just wait. Be patient,' Betty warned.

One for Betty and one for George.

Suddenly Kylie leapt from her seat and rummaged through the presents at the bottom of the tree. She pulled out a large gift, beautifully wrapped with bows and ribbons. 'This is from me and Uncle Wayne,' she said and handed it to the children.

George looked bewildered for a moment but got back to the job.

The children tore at the wrapping paper. Great wafts of it floated around the base of the tree as George, unperturbed, sifted through for the next present.

'Wow! Totem tennis.'

'We can set it up and play later,' Kylie told them.

'Now! Let's do it now!' Jack shouted.

'Later,' Betty told them. 'You have more presents and then there's dinner.'

Wayne held up a pair of sports socks. 'Thanks, Mum. Just what I need.'

Why would Wayne ever need sports anything? The closest he ever got to sport was a bit of elbow exercise while he watched his footy team on the telly.

Janet opened the present on her lap. A coral-pink T shirt. She sighed. She never wore pink. Red was her colour. Burgundy or plum; in fact, any type of red at all.

'Thanks, Mum. It's lovely.' She would have to wear it of course. She'd pop it on next week when Betty came over, so she could see her in it. Then it would be washed, ironed, folded, put away in the bottom drawer and forgotten.

'Not more bloody talcum powder,' Uncle Billy grunted from his seat. 'Will you look at this.' He pointed down to a pile of toiletries on the floor. 'I 'aven't even got through last year's.'

You want to use it more often, thought Janet.

'You want to use it more often,' said Kylie.

Janet looked wide-eyed at Kylie. Betty, who was folding discarded wrapping paper, stopped in her tracks. John chuckled. Wayne leaned forward in his chair.

'More often?' Uncle Billy asked.

'Yes. Don't save it for best. Use it every day when you have a shower or a bath. You shouldn't save up your luxuries.'

'I don't bathe every day.'

'Well, you should.'

There was a pause. *Joy to the World* rang out of the speakers. Everyone waited. Even the children stopped moving, sensing that something important was taking place.

'Then you'll smell delicious. Look at this one.' She held up a bottle. 'This is for the bath. When you use this, you'll not only smell delicious, you'll also feel relaxed. It's very good if you have any aches and pains.'

Uncle Billy rubbed his neck and shoulder with a large, knotty hand. He was always complaining of aches and pains.

'And this one,' Kylie continued, 'this is a roll-on deodorant so you can use it any time. Here, try some. I love the fragrance.'

Uncle Billy seemed totally mesmerised by Kylie's attention. He watched her unwrap the little bottle and unscrew the lid. He looked at it as if it were a foreign object.

No one spoke.

Kylie lifted her arm and pretended to roll deodorant under it. Uncle Billy raised his arm, releasing a gust of putrid underarm odour.

Kylie stood her ground and nodded encouragingly as he rolled it under one arm and then the other. 'That's the way,' she said with a big smile. 'Now try it on your skin.'

Uncle Billy unbuttoned the top button of his shirt and rolled it under each arm. A communal sigh of relief went around the room and everyone got back to what they were doing. Apart from Kylie, who squatted down next to Uncle Billy and chatted some more.

'Thanks, Sis,' Wayne called, holding up a T-shirt.

'You're welcome,' Janet said. Did she buy it? She couldn't remember.

'Bit big now but.' He patted his belly.

She realised then that his beer gut had shrunk.

'Better give it to old Jonno.'

'Less of the old, you cheeky bastard. You're older than me.'

'Yes, Wayne, you're forty!' Janet thought she had better add that for Kylie's benefit. Does she realise how old he is?

'You old bugger.' Kylie jabbed him affectionately in the ribs.

'Well, you know what they say, you're as old as the woman you feel. So, mate, that makes you a damn sight older than me.'

John laughed.

Janet screwed up a large piece of Christmas paper and threw it at Wayne. 'You bastard!'

Betty glared at Janet for the second time that day then turned her attention to the parcel in her lap. 'I'll just open this and then I best get on with the dinner.' She peeled the tape off carefully so as not to tear the paper. Betty believed in recycling. She had always been frugal.

'Thank you, Janet. It's lovely.' She held up a coral-pink T-shirt, not unlike the one she was wearing and very similar to the one that Janet herself had received.

Janet smiled and wondered if she had also bought the T-shirt Betty was wearing. Was it last year's Christmas gift? She looked down at the pink T-shirt she had received. Did Betty assume that Janet liked this colour and style because that's what she always bought for Betty? Perhaps, and this was even more worrying, perhaps it was a recycled present, one that she had given to Betty some other Christmas. Janet felt surreal. It was as if they were living the same Christmas over and over.

'Come on, kids, let's set up the totem tennis.' Kylie jumped up and grabbed the box. 'Bring some music, Wayne,' she said and raced out with the kids trailing after her.

George looked concerned. 'They haven't opened all their presents.'

'They can do it later, Dad.' Janet patted him on the shoulder. She knew her mother wouldn't be happy.

Outside, Wayne and John were arguing about the best place to put the totem tennis pole. They eventually decided that it would be best in the shade of the jacaranda near the fish pond. The children picked up plastic yellow bats and tried to hit the tennis ball on the string. Kylie turned the music on and then leapt up to show the children how to play. She stood behind Natalie and helped her with the bat. As the ball came, they hit it together. John helped Jack and between the four of them they managed to get the ball moving.

'Nice, isn't she?' Wayne said as he stood and watched them play.

'She is. Great with kids and old men.'

'She's a nurse. Works in a nursing home so she's had plenty of practice.'

'She doesn't look old enough.'

'She's twenty-six.'

'She looks like a teenager.'

Wayne laughed. 'You're just getting old.'

'Jeez, it's hot.' John trotted over. 'Just gonna get another beer.' He handed Janet the bat.

Kylie gave her bat to Wayne. 'Here, you two have a go.' She turned up the music, grabbed the children's hands and they danced and sang loudly to *Jingle Bells*.

Janet stood awkwardly with the bat in hand. When was the last time she'd played ball? When was the last time she played anything? Wayne was right, she was getting old. Old and set in her ways like her parents.

She threw the ball up and swung the bat hard. She missed. She tried three times before she got it going. Wayne returned it each time. Maybe she'd underestimated his sporting abilities after all. Thinking about it, he was looking pretty good.

Betty stood with her hands on her wide hips and shouted, 'Dinner is served!' There was an edge to her voice. It was that martyred voice she always put on when things weren't going her way.

In the kitchen, the air conditioner hummed and stirred the smell of roast turkey. George stood carving a large leg of ham. Uncle Billy's rumbling snores could be heard from the lounge.

Kylie looked down at the immaculate table and clapped her hands. 'Betty, this is absolutely beautiful!'

There were Christmas crackers, Christmas napkins, Christmas napkin holders, Christmas candles and a Christmas cake in the middle of the table. Betty laid out her best Royal Doulton china, crystal glasses and silver cutlery. Everything gleamed and sparkled.

'Well, thank you, Kylie,' Betty ran a hand through her grey perm and flushed.

'And look at all this food!'

As always, Betty had prepared roast turkey, roast potatoes, roast vegetables, steamed vegetables, ham, cranberry sauce, apple sauce and gravy. And there was Christmas pudding with brandy custard and cream to follow.

Janet held Betty's small fleshy hand and gave it a little squeeze. 'Mum does this every year,' she told Kylie. 'We're very lucky.'

Betty smiled briefly then pulled out Janet's chair. Janet sat down in her allocated seat while Betty positioned the children either side of her, then went off to usher Uncle Billy from the lounge.

Kylie sat down in the seat opposite Janet. 'I love Christmas, especially when it's so festive like this.'

Janet smiled. She had always thought of Christmas as a day to get through.

Betty arrived with Uncle Billy, who had drool oozing down his craggy chin. 'Kylie, you can't sit there. That's Uncle Billy's seat,' she said firmly.

Kylie looked confused.

'We have our names on the cards,' Janet told Kylie and pointed to the little card in front of her.

'Oh, I'm sorry,' she said. 'Where's mine?'

Betty smiled and pointed to Kylie's place.

Kylie leaned over and promptly swapped the name tags. 'There,' she said. 'All fixed.'

Betty froze, wide-eyed and tight-lipped. Janet thought she looked a little like a startled wombat.

Uncle Billy sat down in his newly allocated seat and stuffed a large portion of bread roll into his mouth. 'Hurry up with that food,' he called.

Janet winced as spit-sodden breadcrumbs spewed from his mouth. 'All right, Mum?' she asked.

Betty composed herself and nodded. She picked up Uncle Billy's napkin, wiped drool and bread crumbs from his chin then tucked the napkin into the front of his shirt. 'George, open that wine when you've finished the meat.'

George continued to cut the meat into neat slices.

Kylie offered her Christmas cracker across the table for Janet to pull.

'You're not allowed to pull crackers now,' Natalie told Kylie. 'We do that after dinner, don't we, Nanna?'

'That's right.'

Janet glanced at her mother's stony face and then at Kylie, who continued to offer the cracker. She smiled, grabbed the end firmly and pulled hard. They both cheered and laughed as the cracker exploded and the contents flew out.

Standing Tall

Damien trudges up the dirt driveway, making small clouds of dust as he goes. He walks around the back, navigating his way between the rubbish – the boxes of empty beer bottles, the old fridge and washer, the rolled-up carpets and discarded car parts. He enters the shitty-nappy smell of the laundry then slips through the door leading to the kitchen. He closes it soundlessly behind him, being careful not to draw attention to himself. The house smells of tobacco and beer. On the grey laminate table an ashtray overflows alongside four empty bottles of beer. A blanket of cigarette smoke floats in the air. The television blares from the lounge room. Marcus is home.

Damien tiptoes to his room and quietly shuts the door behind him. The blind is closed and when he flicks on the light, it brightens to a dreary yellow. He tosses his backpack onto a pile of clothes in the corner of his room and collapses onto his bed. He begins to relax, to allow himself to sink into the soft mattress. He decides to stay in his room till dinner time, to wait until his mum comes home and calls him, but the baby, Jamie, starts crying, softly at first but then louder.

Damien's door flies open and a shadow crosses him.

Marcus leans over, stinking of beer and stale cigarettes. 'You woke the baby!'

Damien grips his quilt cover and feels a prickle pulse down him like an electric shock.

'What have I told you?'

'I didn't,' Damien mumbles.

'What?' Marcus leans in close.

'I didn't mean to.' Damien corrects himself. There's no point arguing, it only makes things worse.

Marcus glares at him for a minute more and then staggers away. On the way out he trips and crashes into the chest of drawers. Damien's baseball bat rolls onto the floor.

'What the fuck!' Marcus spins around and leaps at Damien. 'What have I told you about leaving your shit lying around?' Two massive hands seize Damien's windcheater, lift him from the bed so his nose is touching and Damien can see his own terrified eyes reflected in Marcus's pupils. 'You're fucken useless.'

The baby begins to scream. Marcus tosses Damien down to the bed and continues to hover over him. Strands of greasy hair hang like rat's tails into his bloodshot eyes. Damien is too scared to breathe in case it sets Marcus off. He stays very still as if trying to camouflage himself against the bed but Marcus's gaze is fixed on him and something is running through his head. His eyes narrow and he snatches Damien up by the arms, pulls him clear of the bed and hurls him to the floor.

Damien lands with a thump. His head cracks on the side of the bed and he curls into a ball just as Marcus's boot connects with his back. Damien gasps and another boot connects with his thigh.

The front door slams and Marcus staggers away. Damien lies there nursing his pain, smelling the dust of the carpet and staring at the dark space beneath his bed. He wishes he could crawl into the darkness and never return.

'What the hell did you do that for?' Marcus shouts at Damien's mother. 'I told you what to do.'

She mumbles something back.

'I made it fucken clear enough.'

She mumbles again.

'Don't speak to me like that. I fucken told you.'

There's a scream and something smashes. Damien lies there listening to the sound of his mother being pushed and pulled and another pain starts up. His heart feels as if it is being pierced by a needle. He gets up, leaves the dusty carpet and opens the door a crack. He watches Marcus slap his mother across the face with the back of his hand. She flies back, crashes into the fridge and collapses to the floor. The bottles on top of the fridge shake and rattle.

Marcus staggers about a bit then stands there with his hands on his hips. 'Go and shut that fucken baby up.'

She doesn't move.

'Now!' Marcus sends his steel-capped work boot into her thigh.

Damien sees the same terrified eyes that he saw reflected in Marcus's pupils earlier. He wants to help but he's paralysed; his legs feel as if they have taken root in the ground.

The baby screams like a tortured cat.

'Je-sus!' Marcus smacks his forehead with the palm of his hand. 'Shut up!' he yells in the direction of the baby's room and then staggers toward it. 'I'll shut him up.'

'No!' Damien's mum seizes one of Marcus's legs and hangs on.

He breaks free and she leaps up, pulls at his arm. 'I'll do it. Leave him…'

Marcus punches her in the side of the face and she crashes back onto the kitchen table. Damien reels as if he himself has been punched. His mother clambers up, races after Marcus. Damien seizes the baseball bat and runs into the baby's room. Marcus has his hands around her throat.

'Let go!' Damien holds the bat up. Stands as tall as his thirteen-year-old body will let him. 'Now!' he yells above the baby.

Marcus's fingers relax and she breaks free, races to pick the baby up from the basinet. Marcus stares hard at Damien for a long time and Damien stares back. He doesn't move, doesn't blink. Something changes in Marcus's eyes and he smirks. He takes a cigarette from his shirt pocket, lights it, has a long drag and blows smoke out through his nose. He swaggers out of the room, grabs the car keys from the kitchen table and heads out the front door, giving it a hard slam behind him.

Meeting the In-laws

George shuts the door of the guest room and walks into the open-spaced kitchen and family room.

'You look nice. Very smart,' Jane, his daughter-in-law, says.

'Thank you.' He smooths his freshly pressed shirt and straightens his navy tie. His black shoes are polished and shiny and his trousers have sharp pleats. Having travelled all the way to Australia from the motherland to meet his new family, he must look his absolute best and make a good impression.

'Are you sure you'll be comfortable?' Jane asks. 'It is thirty-eight degrees out there still. You might be a little hot.'

'Lord, no. I'll be fine. I'm dressed for dinner.'

'It's just a barbecue tea,' Jane says.

George checks his watch and Jane grates a carrot for the coleslaw.

'They'll be here soon,' George says and nods to the salad. 'You don't have much time.'

'It's almost done.' She smiles.

'And you still have to get ready.'

'Sorry?' Jane stops grating carrot and looks up at George.

'Dressed. You still have to get dressed.'

'I am dressed.'

'Yes. I mean… I can see you're dressed,' George says in his best BBC English so she can fully comprehend, 'but surely you need to get changed.' He looks down at her pink rubber flip-flops.

Jane tosses a piece of carrot into her mouth and crunches loudly.

These Australians are barbaric, he thinks. 'For dinner,' he adds.

'It's a barbecue,' she tells him and vigorously grates the remaining carrot.

'I'll let you get ready then,' he says and heads out the patio door.

George sits outside in the drooping evening wondering how the birds can sound so cheerful in the heat. He straightens his tie and tugs his shirt collar a little.

'Are you all right, dear?' his wife Rosemary asks.

'Yes. I'm fine. Just making sure my skin hasn't melted in this abominable heat. How do they stand it?'

The sliding door opens and Dave trots out wearing shorts, sandals and T-shirt. 'I thought I'd get the barby going,' he tells them, carrying a plate. 'I know how you like to eat early.'

George gets up and stands next to the barbecue. He pulls back the tea towel over the plate. 'Very Australian,' he says glancing at the chops and sausages.

'Grab a beer, Dad.' Dave nods to the small esky next to the barbecue.

George bends, takes a small bottle of beer out and opens it. There are no glasses so he heads into the kitchen to get one. The doorbell rings and Jane rushes past to answer it. George takes the glass outside and pours himself a beer.

Shortly after, the patio door opens.

'Mum, Dad,' Jane says, 'I'd like you to meet Dave's parents, George and Rosemary.'

George is momentarily frozen. Jane's father is Asian! He grasps the extended brown hand with his large white one.

'G'day,' Jane's father says. 'I'm Greg and this is my lovely wife, Margy.'

George nods. 'Greg. Margaret.'

'Call me Margy.'

'Right, yes. Right. Well, this is a surprise. Dave didn't tell me that his father-in-law is a foreigner. That makes two of us.'

There's a pause. Even the barbecue stops spitting.

Greg takes the beer offered by Dave. 'Cheers,' he says and smiles. 'My father was Chinese.'

'But Jane doesn't look it. She looks as white as a sheet.'

'Takes after her mother,' Greg says. 'And I'm only half Asian. My mother was Australian.' He laughs good-heartedly and twists the top off his beer.

Dave adds the onions to the barbecue plate. The air is thick with the smell of searing meat.

'So how are you enjoying our beautiful country so far?' Greg asks.

'It's very quaint. Rosemary and I are quite delighted, aren't we, dear?'

Rosemary nods and smiles.

'I never thought I'd ever visit. It's not really a place that had ever enticed me.'

'No? Why's that? Australia's a beautiful country.'

'Well, yes, Margaret, I can see that now.'

'Call me Margy.'

'What? Oh yes.' George swats at a fly. 'But I never would have found that out. All I'd ever heard about were the flies, the snakes and spiders. And I remember all those dreadful adverts.'

'Adverts?'

'Yes, you know, from long ago, that awful man with the blond hair. "Throw another shrimp on the barby",' George says in an Australian twang. 'And then there was the latest one. The one that hit the news. What was that?'

'Where the bloody hell are you?' Jane offers.

'Yes, that one. It made us all squirm. Didn't it, dear?'

Rosemary smiles.

'So common.'

The barbecue flares and chops sizzle.

'Common?' Greg chuckles.

'Yes, if our son hadn't married a colonial girl, we wouldn't have bothered to come. What do they call it? The land of the savages.' He tugs the collar of his shirt to let some air in.

Greg slaps his thigh and laughs.

George begins to hum the tune of *The Wild Colonial Boy*. 'How does it go?' He warms up his voice and sings in an impressive baritone, 'She was her father's only hope, her mother's only joy…'

'That's very good. You've got a great voice,' Greg says. 'But my girl, she's more than that. Aren't you, Janey?'

Jane smiles. 'Yes, indeed I am.'

'Oh?' George is confused.

'She's not just a colonial.' Greg draws quotes in the air. 'She's the real deal. You see Margy and myself are Aboriginal.' He grins a white-toothed grin.

'Good Lord!' George says. 'But…you just told me you're Asian.'

'Only half Asian. Half Australian too. Aboriginal. And Margy here, she's half herself.'

'Surely not! She's fair. Her skin and hair…even her eyes.'

Greg shrugs. 'That's the way the old Aboriginal cookie crumbles sometimes.'

George thinks this must be a joke but only Greg is smiling. 'You're serious?'

'Yep.'

'So that means…'

'That means your daughter-in-law is one part English, one part Asian and two parts savage.' He cackles.

'Meat's done,' Dave calls. 'Come and help yourself.'

Greg stands up. 'Come on, mate. Let's go and get a barbecued witchetty grub.' He winks and George feels himself shrink like an overcooked piece of steak.

After dinner, Jane places a large dessert in the middle of the slatted wooden table.

'Good Lord. Will you look at that, Rosemary.'

'Yes. It looks delicious.'

'What do you call that then?' George asks. 'It looks like a giant meringue with fruit.'

'It's a pav,' Greg says.

'A pav?'

'A pavlova.'

'Oh, like the famous ballet dancer?' George asks.

'Exactly. It was named after her, in actual fact.'

'Well, very nice. We'll enjoy tasting that, won't we, Rosemary? A bit of culinary Australia.'

'The old pav has had some controversy in its time,' Greg tells them.

Jane slices the pavlova carefully but the thick crusty meringue crumbles. She scoops it up and passes a large bowl to George.

'Thank you. I hope I can eat it all.'

'She's trying to sweeten you up, mate,' Greg says. 'Just a little one for me, Janey.'

George spoons in a large mouthful and lets the sweetness dissolve on his tongue. 'Delicious. These Australians have got the food right at least,' he says. 'So tell me, Greg, about this controversy.'

'Well, the pav was invented back in the 1920s when Anna Pavlova toured Australia and New Zealand. And no one really knows whether it was actually the Aussies or the Kiwis who invented it. The earliest recipe so far, dated in 1929, was found in New Zealand.'

'Fascinating.'

'Yep. I love a bit of history, don't you?'

'Absolutely. In fact, it was my dream as a boy to go to Oxford to study history.'

'What a coincidence,' Jane says. 'Dad's a history teacher, or was. Weren't you, Dad?'

'Yes ,indeed I was.'

'Really a teacher?' George loads his spoon. 'I hadn't actually got you pegged as a teacher.'

'No?'

'You've got a BA then, or a teacher's certificate?'

'No, no,' Jane says. 'Dad's a lecturer. He's got a PhD in history.'

'Really?' George is astounded. He sucks in some air with his pavlova and the powdery crust tickles his throat. He coughs violently. 'Excuse me,' he gasps.

'George always wanted to be a history master but his father made him study accounting,' he hears Rosemary tell them as he heads inside for a glass of water.

The cool chlorinated water soothes his throat. He sighs. A PhD. A lecturer. A history lecturer. He feels himself droop like a sapling gum on a hot day.

After a few minutes, he feels a little better and goes back outside. 'Sorry about that. It's very crumbly,' he says. 'I'd best not have any more. Very nice, though. Very nice.'

'Have another beer, Dad.' Dave offers him a stubby.

George takes it, twists off the lid then looks around. 'Where's my glass?' he asks.

'You don't need all those airs and graces now,' Greg says. 'You're in Australia. Relax.' Greg raises his stubby of beer and demonstrates how to drink it.

'Here.' Dave passes George a foam stubby holder and he slides the bottle in.

'Cheers,' says Greg. 'Welcome to the land of Oz.'

Rosemary hands George a serviette. 'Wipe your face, dear.' She pats a spot on her cheek to indicate where George is wearing food.

'Huh?'

'You've got some pavlova…a bit of meringue on your face,' Jane says.

George dabs his face with the paper serviette.

'It's made of egg, you know,' Greg tells him.

'Egg?'

Greg nods and winks.

'Oh, oh, I see.' George grins. 'Cheers,' he says and lifts the bottle to his lips.

Murder in Underground Road

Underground Road is where you hear screams in the middle of the night and sometimes in the middle of the day. Not long ago, a murderer lived around the corner. He buried seven children under the floorboards in a cellar. You can't see the house now; it's just a vacant lot with scraped red earth. The council sent bulldozers to knock the house down because they said that no one would ever want to live there. Trucks came and carted grey rubble away. When I stood with the quiet crowd of neighbours that gathered to watch, I thought I heard the sound of screaming and whenever I saw a flash of white, I wondered if it were the glint of bone. I don't like cellars or dark corners any more.

My name is Damien. I live with my mum, my older brother, Blake, and my two little sisters, Skye and Kelly. We had a baby brother too, his name was Jamie but he died. Mum is still very sad from Jamie's death, we all are, but Mum is the saddest. She stopped crying a few weeks ago but she doesn't say anything much now. She sits in the lounge and stares ahead at the turned-off TV. Mostly we have to get our own dinner and get ourselves off to school.

Jamie's coffin was so small, it didn't seem big enough for his little body. It didn't seem real. When I watched the shiny, white coffin sink into the ground, I thought of cellars and bone and screaming, and I went to the toilet to be sick.

Our house is like the murder house. It's the same design; a small, grey half-house with three little bedrooms, a lounge, kitchen, laundry and toilet. Blake and I sleep in one bedroom, my sisters sleep in another and Mum and Marcus sleep in the biggest bedroom. Except Marcus doesn't live with us any more. Marcus left when Jamie died.

Jamie used to sleep in Mum's room in a white bassinet. I miss Jamie but I don't miss Marcus and I hope he never comes back.

Jamie was loud like Marcus except he cried and screamed while Marcus shouted and slammed things down. Marcus was so strong he punched a hole in my door. He was mad at me because I couldn't stop crying and I woke up Jamie, who'd only just gone off to sleep. Jamie didn't like to sleep very much. I didn't mean to cry but I fell off my bunk bed and hurt my arm. It still hurts a little now but I won't tell Mum because, if Marcus comes back, she might tell him and he'd be mad at me again.

I went to the murderer's house one day with Blake. The murderer's name was Mr Hobby. I didn't like him. He was tall and thin with black hair sprouting from his nose. I didn't like the way he smiled at me with his broken brown teeth. I went into his house because I wanted to get a present from him. Blake told me that Mr Hobby gave presents if he liked you; he gave Blake a slim silver pocket knife.

Inside, the house was dark because all the blinds were pulled down. The lounge room and kitchen were lit up with yellow bulbs that hung on wire from the ceilings. Long, stringy cobwebs dangled from the corners of the rooms. The house smelt like the kitty-litter box needed emptying but I didn't see a cat or a litter tray. I didn't like the smell or the dark or the cobwebs, so I left even though I would have liked a pocket knife of my own.

Blake loves knives and guns. He has Marcus's rifle and he knows how to use it. He and Marcus went spotlighting a few times to shoot kangaroos and rabbits. Once, they brought home three dead rabbits and Marcus showed us how to skin them. Kelly screamed when she saw the bloody bodies on the concrete step out the back. She hid her guinea pig, Roxie, in her room because she thought Marcus might shoot and skin it. I thought he might too when he slipped on little round balls of guinea pig poo in her bedroom. It made him so angry that he crawled under the bed and tried to pull Roxie out from a dark corner.

Kelly screamed, 'Leave her. I'll get her! She'll come to me. I'll get her!'

Marcus ignored Kelly and inched further under the bed. When the guinea pig squealed, Kelly dropped to the floor and sunk her teeth into Marcus's leg.

I heard his head crack on the metal base of the bed before he clambered out from under it. Kelly checked to see if he had the guinea pig in his hands before she darted from the room. Marcus caught Kelly by her bright red hair, threw her to the floor and slapped her across her face. Three red fingerprints shone on her freckled cheek for the rest of the day and a purple bruise grew where her forehead hit the lino. I don't know what happened to the guinea pig. Kelly didn't talk for a long time after that.

Whenever Marcus got his cheque, he would go out for a big drinking session. Sometimes he wouldn't come home for days. I always felt better when Marcus wasn't home. It was one less person to worry about. Blake was still a problem, though, because when Marcus wasn't home, Blake would take the rifle from the top of Mum's wardrobe and smuggle it into his room. He would sit on his bed and polish it or take out all the bullets then reload.

One day he aimed it at me.

'Don't, Blake!'

'It's not loaded, stupid.'

I thought of the murderer and wondered how a murderer began. Is it something that starts early? Can a gun make a murderer? Blake always looked excited when he held it in his hands.

'Right between the eyes,' he said and steadied the rifle.

Click!

My heart cracked like a gun and made my chest ache.

I must have looked scared because Blake said, 'I told you it's not loaded, idiot.'

'Marcus'll kill you.'

'He'll never know.'

I raised my eyebrows to him, to suggest that I might tell him myself.

'If you say anything, I'll fucking shoot you.' A deep crease appeared between his eyes. 'I mean it.'

I looked away. 'I never would. I never said I would.'

Blake snapped open the rifle, loaded it, snapped it shut then pointed it back at me. 'Right between the fucking eyes.'

I felt sick. I felt as if I was going to throw up. Blake called me a sook and laughed.

I wanted to hit him, to pull him to the ground, to kick him, punch him, whack the rifle butt onto his head. I wanted to hear the sound of his skull crack. But I didn't. I felt as if my limbs were full of concrete. I sat like a statue, with nothing but fear running through my veins and wished he were dead. Right at that moment, I wished with all my heart that Mr Hobby had killed Blake like he killed the other children.

After Jamie died, Marcus sat in the grey recliner chair in the lounge and drank from a flagon for a long time. Whenever he and Mum were in the same room, they argued. On the day that Marcus left, they had a big fight and Mum screamed and screamed. Skye and Kelly hid under the bed. I don't like small, dark spaces so I crouched in the corner of my room with my hands over my ears and hummed 'How Much is that Doggy in the Window?'

Blake wasn't home to listen to it; he was out with his friend Zac. When he came back in the morning, Mum's lips were puffy and there were blue marks on her neck. That's when Blake stole Marcus's gun and hid it under the old brick stand that holds up the rusty rainwater tank. Marcus didn't come home for three days and when he did, he and Mum had another fight. When he packed his stuff and left, he didn't seem to notice the gun was missing. Maybe he thought Mum had hidden it somewhere.

I miss Jamie. I liked coming home from school and seeing him. Mum would ask me to hold him while she cooked dinner and he would squeeze my fingers tightly in his tiny fist. He used to smile at me too and watch me very carefully. I liked the way his blue eyes crossed when he stared at me.

Blake liked Jamie too but he didn't like him when he cried and sometimes he would scream at him to shut up. Just like Marcus did. Mum never shouted at Jamie but she used to go very quiet when he would cry and she would cry with him sometimes. The whole house felt dark when he cried. If Marcus was home, he would start to mutter under his breath and then start to pace and run his fingers through his hair or blow cigarette smoke out through his teeth in a long, low whistle. He'd shout, 'For Christ's sake shut that bloody child up!'

In the beginning, Mum tried harder and rocked Jamie faster or jiggled him up and down and shushed him, but he only ever seemed to cry louder. Then Mum would start crying and Marcus would shout more. We would all go and sit in our rooms with the doors closed and our hands or pillows over our ears.

If Marcus wasn't home and Jamie started to cry, Mum would sometimes leave him to cry alone. On the day that Jamie died, she made herself a cup of tea, lit a cigarette and went outside without him. She sat at the bottom of the garden on the broken swing and stared into nowhere. I felt bad for Mum. She never laughed or even smiled any more. She didn't talk to any of us, just shouted if something needed doing. I wanted to see her smile again. Since Marcus and Jamie, there was nothing but arguing and shouting and guns.

As I watched her from the kitchen window, it felt like I was watching a sad movie. Mum sat quietly outside and the baby screamed in the background. The noise was too much it felt like a dark blanket that cut out the light. I walked into my room, shut the door and leaned against it. I closed my ears with my hands and hummed 'How Much is that Doggy in the Window?' I could still hear Jamie and through my thin white T-shirt, I could feel the hole in the door that Marcus made. I turned and traced a finger around the hole and stared into the dark hollow. I put my fist in; there was plenty of room. Both my fists fit into Marcus's hole and I wondered if my hands would ever be as big as his. Jamie continued to scream.

I opened the door and walked into Mum's room to help Jamie

settle down. I walked in to stop Jamie from crying. I wanted to help
Mum. If Jamie were quiet then Mum would feel better. She might even
start to laugh again. I thought of Mr Hobby as I bent down and looked
at the screaming red-faced Jamie. I thought of Marcus's large hands,
of Marcus's gun, of Blake's knife. I continued to hum 'How Much is
That Doggy?' and gently, very gently, I covered Jamie's little head with
the pillow and gradually, very gradually, he became quiet.

Imagine

You earn two hundred and forty-eight dollars per week. You live on your own in a small two-bedroom unit. You have multiple health problems and require a reasonable diet. You support your children whenever you can. They come to stay every now and again because they're sad or because they miss you or because they are broke. You feed them. You are, after all, a good mother, a caring mother. You couldn't possibly tell them that you can't afford to feed them. They stay a little longer than planned. They use the telephone and hot water. They use more electricity than you would, they heat their room because it's so cold. It's an icy winter. After a few weeks, they leave and get back to the business of independent living.

Shortly after, your electricity bill arrives. It's fifty dollars more than you expected. You have even less money than planned because you spent extra on food when Johnny and Susie came to stay. Once you pay the rent, pay the electricity bill and put aside a little for the gas bill (which is due the following week) you don't have enough for food. You decide to spend the gas money on groceries. After all, you're hungry. You haven't eaten well for weeks. Your health is beginning to worsen. You also stopped the blood pressure medication because you were short last fortnight. You know you shouldn't, but four dollars eighty will buy milk and bread at the discounted bakery.

Before long, the gas bill comes in and it, too, is higher than expected due to the children's visit. You can scrape together sixty dollars but the bill is a hundred and twenty. You decide to leave it for the time being. You stick it to the fridge and try not to think about it. Eventually, you phone the gas company to talk with a customer service officer who tells you your supply will not be disconnected if you pay sixty dollars now and the remainder the following fortnight. You agree, even though you know you won't have the money unless you go without food, because the telephone bill and the ambulance cover have also arrived. You need both. You can't afford for the phone to be cut off. How will you call an ambulance if your health continues to falter? How will you call the police if he breaks in? How will you be able to check that Johnny and Susie are okay? You pay the phone bill and ambulance cover, you buy enough food to last a fortnight and pray nobody comes to stay.

Your gas is disconnected. You feel ashamed so you don't tell anyone. You wonder how you will ever be able to afford to pay the sixty-dollar reconnection fee on top of what you already owe. You decide you can live without gas for a time but you develop a cold rather quickly. Those blankets weren't as thick as you thought. There's nothing to do but take a stroll to the chemist and buy some over-the-counter medication to try to combat your cold. You're frightened it will turn to pneumonia. You've had it once before and your lungs are weak.

You wander to the shops in a dream. How would your children survive without you? They're so fragile. Their father wasn't kind to them. He wasn't kind to you either. You take a tight hold of your coat collar and draw it close to your neck. The wind is chill. The children missed a lot of school with all that fuss going on in the house, all that explosive anger. You didn't have much energy for them. You didn't monitor them well enough, didn't check that they'd gone where they said they would. You begin to weep at the thought of your young children in the hands of the local paedophile at Number Three. People stare as they pass your teary face, your nose is red with cold and grief. Of course, you didn't know he was a paedophile until much later but still, if you had known where they were, if you had not been married to that swine, if the house had been somewhere warm and safe like it is now then maybe, maybe things would be different.

Something shifts in your stomach. The house isn't warm now. What if the children come and the house isn't warm and safe for them? You have to protect them now, even though you couldn't then. You owe them.

There's a sign. Easy Cash. Instant Money. Instant Solutions. You don't even think about it. You just do it out of instinct. You need a way out of this mess and that's what the sign promises to do. Instantly. They want your pension card number. They tell you if you have a pension card, all will be well. Provided you do not have a Mount-Everest-type mountain of debt then you will be fine. You tell them you have a debt with the Housing Trust and one with SA Ambulance. You also owe Centrelink for the advance you received two months ago. You feel your cheeks grow hot as the man behind the desk writes the information down. You want to tell him that they're not your debts. It was that man you married. The one who loved you. He loved you so much that he broke every piece of furniture in the house, knocked holes in the walls and the doors and finally one in your head when you said that you could not live with him any more. It was when you found out about the paedophile. Twenty years after the event. It tore your heart in two. It still does every day. That day you said, Enough! Said you would rather die. Felt you had died. Believed he could not hurt you any more. Nothing could hurt you more than betraying your own children.

But he did hurt you and when the children found your bleeding, unconscious body, they called an ambulance to take you to the hospital. Now you have to repay the debt.

A tear blurs your vision of the man with the pen. He tells you that it is fine. Everything is great. Provided you have the documentation – a couple of bills with your current address, a Centrelink statement and some ID – you can have the money.

It's all there in a crumpled heap in your bag. You feel relief. Feel that tear dry-up in your eye. The man passes you the paperwork to read. You lean over it and pretend to read for a minute. Of course, you can't see it, it's all a blur. Your eyesight is not what it used to be and you don't have a decent pair of glasses to see such small type. You nod to the man and hand the contract back. He doesn't seem to notice that you can't read it. He offers you a pen and points at a space for you to sign. He tells you with your income you can borrow eighty dollars. He tells you that you'll be able to borrow more next time once you have shown that you can make repayments on time. He tells you the repayments will come out of your pension. You won't miss it, he says. Only sixty-four eighty per fortnight for two fortnights and then you're done. You can have the money right now, he says, and offers you four crisp twenty-dollar notes which you put deep inside your purse.

You go to the chemist and buy some medication for your cold but you already feel better. Tomorrow, when you receive your pension, you'll have enough to have the gas reconnected. The thought of having the money to pay the gas bill and warm your home makes you feel lighter. You manage a smile. You do something extraordinary: you sit down in the café and have a leisurely cappuccino and a custard tart and wonder why you've never thought to borrow money before.

The next day, you pay your gas bill and the man comes to reconnect. You feel a sense of achievement for having got out of this mess all by yourself. The flat warms slowly and you shed your coat. Your cold has eased, the sinus ache has gone and you can breathe easier. Your lungs are not so wheezy either.

You have a good week. Now that your bills are paid, you feel happier. You help your neighbour, Rhonda, with her shopping. She had a nasty fall last week and has a badly bruised leg. She doesn't feel able to walk to the local shops to buy food. She provides you with a list, her eftpos card and her pin number. She has no cash in the house and she knows she can trust you. You're happy to help Rhonda. She has helped you many times in the past. She phoned the police to report a prowler peering in your window that night your husband returned. She didn't know he was your husband, you didn't tell her. You just thanked her because you didn't hear the slicing of the flywire, the lifting of the sash window. Nor did you see the workman's boot ease its way into the lounge room. If you had, you might have had a stroke. All the memories, all the fear from the past, would have immobilised you like a rabbit or a roo caught in a spotlight. You would have been dead meat.

Now you have a security system. You have to for your own safety. It's not cheap but it's something that you cannot be without. The police could not lock him up for long and restraining orders don't mean much. Not to a violent, obsessed man. You often wonder if he'll wait for you around the corner of your house. You wonder if he'll take you as you walk the pavement to the local shops, or whether he'll bide his time and wait for you to falter on the security system payments.

As you walk down the lane towards the shopping centre, you notice your palms are sweating despite the icy cold. You look around anxiously. Surely, he wouldn't seize you here in broad daylight? You gather your coat to your chest and try not to think about him, which is difficult because you've spent most of your life with him. Your freedom is new even though you don't really feel free. You have the Housing Trust and ambulance debts and you have the furniture repayments from Radio Rentals because you had to replace the table and chairs that he smashed to bits. They were very easy to get at Radio Rentals with your pension card but sometimes it is difficult to find that much money each month for the repayments.

At the supermarket, there's a gang of youths. You see these youths often. You don't like them. They're unpredictable. Sometimes they appear drunk but maybe they're on drugs. They are hanging around the ATM. Rhonda asked you to buy some food and cigarettes for her. She also wants you to take out fifty dollars. You decide to do that in the supermarket. Decide to avoid the youths at the teller machine. You walk into the shop with Rhonda's list and avoid eye contact with any of them. Inside, you relax and begin to walk the narrow aisles in the gloomy light in search of the items on Rhonda's list. You get her the home brand where possible because you know it will be cheaper and Rhonda can't afford to buy luxuries any more than you can.

You put the items in the little green shopping basket and go to the check-out. The girl behind the counter chews gum and doesn't look at you. She laughs loudly as one of the youths is pushed and skitters through the doorway. You ask the girl for fifty dollars in cash but in ten-dollar notes. You know Rhonda likes to divide her money this way. The girl chews open-mouthed and hands you the machine. You slide the card into the slot, squint your eyes to see the buttons and carefully punch in the numbers. She gives you the money with the receipt and then the bags of groceries.

You put the money in your coat pocket and take the bags toward the door. The youths are still there with their noise and shuffling. One bumps you. You are small and very thin. Once you were wiry and strong but now you're just skin and bone. The knock is not absorbed and you falter. A bag of groceries falls to the ground. You think you're going down too but a youth catches you and puts you upright again. He gives you a warm smile. You're relieved you didn't fall. At your age, with your bones, you could easily crack something. The youths pick up your groceries for you. You thank them and feel a pang of guilt because of your first impression of them. You feel queasy from the knock and the commotion and walk slowly home.

When you arrive back at Rhonda's, she greets you at the door. She's dying for a cigarette, she tells you. She takes the groceries, digs out the small packet of Escort Blue and tears off the outer wrapping. You chat about the youths as you put a tin of cat food and a bag of sugar in her cupboard. You take the money out of your pocket and leaf through the notes out of habit. You immediately notice the missing ten-dollar note. Your stomach plunges and your heart fires up as you fumble around in your pocket. It's not there. You look all around your feet and toward the door in case it fell out when you walked in but there's nothing on the grey lino except a small brown cat biscuit.

Rhonda doesn't notice. She has taken her cigarette and her silver ashtray into the tiny lounge room and sits with her bruised leg propped up as she inhales deeply. You feel inside your pocket again but of course there is nothing there. You bend and look under the table. Nothing. You cast your mind back to the shop. Perhaps the girl didn't give you all the notes. You don't remember checking to see if the money was all there. Perhaps it fell from your coat pocket when you were jostled by the youths. Perhaps that nice youth, the one who caught you, perhaps he took it. Your mood plummets as you realise that it's gone and there is nothing else to do but give Rhonda ten dollars from your own purse. You take out two crumpled five-dollar notes and leave them on the table with her money. You make Rhonda a cup of tea and a ham sandwich, and say goodbye.

You decide to go back to the shop and look for the ten dollars. You can't afford to lose that much money. You can buy food for two days with ten dollars, maybe three if you're very careful. Outside, the icy wind has strengthened and you realise that if you had dropped the note it would have blown away. Still, you must look.

The supermarket girl stops chewing briefly as you tell your story. She shakes her head when you ask if it's possible that she only gave you forty dollars instead of fifty. You want to say that if there is an extra ten dollars in the till at the end of the day to put it aside for you. You want to give her your telephone number just in case someone finds your money and hands it in but you feel ashamed of your desperation. To her, ten dollars is nothing more than a lost packet of cigarettes. Easily replaced. There is no sign of the youths inside or outside the shop. There is no sign of your cash either. You head home with your nose streaming, the bottom of your grey coat flapping and your hands clutching your thick woollen collar.

At home, you lock yourself in. Your energy is spent. You have some cold and flu medication and warm a tin of home-brand soup for your dinner. You turn the gas heating down and flick off all the lights. Every penny counts. You turn on the TV, snuggle down under your quilt and let the mug of soup warm you. Eventually you drift into a heavy, fitful sleep. You dream it is pension day. You dream that the money you owe the loan company comes out at the same time as the money for the security system, the Radio Rentals payment and your rent. Your health deteriorates. Your airways are moist and raspy.

You have a fever and become delirious. You dream that the following fortnight on pension day, your bank account is overdrawn and there is a thirty-eight dollar dishonour fee and not enough money in the account for the security system. You live in a state of panic in case the system is disconnected. You dream your electricity is cut off. You dream you saw a face at the window. You dream your letterbox is filling with bills and debt collection notices that you take inside and hide under your mattress because you can't bear to look at them. You dream that someone tries to break-in. You dream and dream and when the fever finally lifts, you realise there was no dream.

In Our Street

In our street, in Underground Road, an ambulance came and took Mrs Winter away. She was dead. Rayleen and I watched as the ambulance men carried the stretcher through her front door and down the gravel driveway to the van. I knew she was dead because her face was covered with a white sheet and I saw one of her hands hang down as if she were asleep.

'I think she was murdered,' I told Rayleen as I swung my hips to get the hula hoop going.

'No she wasn't! She just died of old age.' Rayleen said when people get really old, as old as one hundred like Mrs Winter, they start to crack and then their hearts crack and then they die. Rayleen always knew things.

Mrs Winter was the oldest person in our street, the oldest person I had ever known. And she was cracking; her face looked like the cracked mud at the bottom of a dry puddle. But I thought she was murdered. Murder happened a lot in our street and in our family. So why would Mrs Winter be any different?

It started with Blackie. Blackie was my cat; everyone said so. She was a small cat and she was black. I used to dress her up and put her in my doll's pram and walk her up and down the street to show the neighbours. And they would say, 'What a lovely baby. What's her name?' And I'd tell them it was Blackie sometimes; other times I would tell them it was Cat or Catty. They thought that was funny.

Blackie was beautiful and she never scratched me. Rayleen said that's a good way to tell if a cat loves you. That and if they lick you. Blackie was my best friend, better even than Rayleen.

The day she died, Peter, my brother, ran into the kitchen and yelled, 'Dad's murdering the cat!'

I raced out to save Blackie but Mum caught me and swung me around and stopped me from going any further. I wriggled and squirmed and yelled until Dad came from the back of the garden. He had a shovel over his shoulder and a mean look on his face.

'Murderer!' I screamed.

He knelt down next to me and said, 'I didn't want to kill Blackie. She got hit by a car and I had to put her out of her misery.'

'Smacked the shovel right on her head!' Peter told me.

Later, Dad went to the bottom of the garden and dug a big hole to put Blackie in. When he finished, we all went to the funeral. There was a big earth mound under the nectarine tree where Blackie was buried. Dad made a small cross out of two bits of wood and I put it on her grave with some red geraniums. Then Dad said a prayer and told me that Blackie would go to heaven, where she would be happy forever more.

Blackie might have been happy but I missed her and visited her grave every day. I sat on the prickly buffalo grass with the smell of rotting nectarines and talked to Blackie as if she were there and not on her way to heaven.

Mum and Dad bought a dog, a little Australian terror. She was very small, smaller even than Blackie was, which was funny because dogs chase cats so they should be bigger. I called her Brownie because she was brown and black but mostly brown. Everyone else called her Tammy. I liked Brownie and I knew she liked me because she licked me but she didn't like to play the same games as Blackie. She jumped out of the pram and I wasn't allowed to take her out of the yard to visit the neighbours.

I asked if I could have another cat but Mum and Dad said, 'No. No more cats.' They bought me two little pet mice instead.

The little mice were very cute. I used to get them out of their big wooden cage and play with them on the red concrete step at the front of the house. I taught them to do tricks like Mum did with Brownie. They had silky white fur, pink ears, pink tails and red beady eyes.

Not everyone liked my pet mice. Uncle Bob, Auntie Mary and my cousins from the farm hated them. They called them vermin. There was a plague in the country that year and the ground had turned to mice. When my uncle flicked on the spotlight at night, the ground moved and swayed like a grey sea. My cousins put on their big black boots and ran over the top of them, crunching their bones. Even the farmhouse cats were tired of mice. They got fat and lay around and let mice run and jump all over them.

I called my mice Whitey and Pinky but I didn't know which was which because they looked exactly the same. Dad said he couldn't tell the difference either but said there must have been a big difference because one was a boy and one was a girl and they got married and had eight pink babies.

Dad made another cage to put the father in because otherwise he would eat the babies. The babies were not cute. They were bald, had slitty eyes and flat little ears. Rayleen said that's why the father wanted to eat them – because they were so ugly.

The new cage was made of wood too. It had an upstairs and downstairs, a cubby-hole to hide in and a big wooden door on the back with a silver hinge. I was sure Eric would like it. (Eric was the new name I gave the mouse when he moved because Peter said it wasn't imaginative to call animals by their colours.) But when I showed Eric his new home, he didn't like it. I put him in and he ran back towards me. I thought he might be trying to get out, to get to the babies, so I slammed the door shut and trapped his neck. When I opened the door he rolled about for a long time with big, bulgy eyes. He finally stopped with his little pink feet in the air. That's how I murdered Eric.

I was very sad and cried for a long time but Dad reminded me that he would go to heaven and live happily ever after and that made me feel better. Dad said we would bury him next to Blackie. He got the shovel and told me to hold Eric while he dug the hole. I held his warm little body and stroked his silky fur and thought it would be better if he had a coffin to be buried in. That way, his lovely white coat wouldn't get all dirty. I got an empty jam jar from the kitchen cupboard, put him inside and screwed the lid on tight. I carried him carefully to the nectarine tree where Dad had dug a hole. I put the coffin in the hole and Dad covered it over. I cried for a long time. I didn't like being a murderer even if Eric was going to be happier up in heaven. I put a pink geranium on Eric's grave and said a prayer.

I dreamed of cats and mice every night after that. I thought that Blackie would be chasing Eric in heaven because cats and mice don't like each other and cats eat mice. Rayleen said that wouldn't happen because cats go to Cat Heaven and mice go to Mice Heaven.

I still dreamed of them every night till the wild, grey mouse came to visit. If he were my mouse, I would have called him Smoke or Ash because they are the colour of grey and that would be imaginative. But he wasn't my mouse and he gave me a fright when he ran up my bed and over my pillow and under my covers. I screamed so loud that Mum and Dad came and so did Brownie. When Dad lifted the covers, Brownie dived in and there was growling and shaking. Then she came out and dropped the little mouse at my feet. She was trembling and her eyes were so wide they glinted like marbles. I looked down at the little mouse at my feet; its black eyes had popped and its body was crushed. Brownie murdered it but it was my fault for screaming.

That night the Pied Piper visited me in my bedroom. He played on his golden pipe and marched on the spot in his tight blue clothes with his pointy black boots. I screamed but my voice was empty and I was too frightened to get up and go to Mum and Dad's room so I hid my head under the covers with the smell of dog and mouse. Some time that night I went to sleep.

The next day Peter told me that he saw the mouse lying on top of a pile of rubbish in the incinerator. I didn't want Smoke to turn into his name so I rescued him. I wanted to give him a funeral and bury him in the mouse grave with Eric. I knew there would be room there because Eric would already be in heaven like Blackie. So I dug up the grave.

I found the jar, the coffin, all covered in dirt. The lid was on tight,

I snapped it open and out flew a stiff wet mouse with thorny fur. It frightened me and I ran back into the house and hid under my bed.

At teatime I asked, 'What happens to you if you don't go to heaven?'

Peter said, 'You go to hell.'

The next day, Rayleen told me that you mustn't bury things in glass because the ants and bugs can't get to them and it's the flying ants that take the bits up to heaven. I hoped it wasn't too late for Eric.

I never played with the other mice after that; the babies grew up and they all lived together. I used to visit them sometimes but I didn't get them out in case I murdered another one.

Then, one day, I went to visit them and they were all dead. The door was open and there was a box near the cage. I didn't tell anyone but that night I heard Mum say to Dad that my cousin from the farm probably crushed them.

'Just doing his job,' she said.

I was sad that Eric's babies were dead but glad that someone else had murdered them and was responsible for getting them to heaven.

I wondered who had murdered Mrs Winter and who'd be responsible for getting her to heaven. She didn't have many visitors. Mrs Winter's visitors all wore suits or uniforms and sad faces.

I didn't know Mrs Winter very well but I did visit her house twice. The first time was when I was taking Blackie to visit the neighbours. Pat and Valerie weren't home so I walked up Mrs Winter's gravel driveway and knocked on her door instead. I stood there for ages waiting for her to answer. I knew she was home; I saw her sitting at the window as I walked in through the gate.

She was always at her window looking out over our street and her little garden. It wasn't a real garden like our garden with green grass and roses and geraniums. Mrs Winter's grass was patchy and in the summer it was yellow like straw. She did have an oleander bush in the corner and that was pretty. Sometimes I would pick one of the giant flowers and put it in my hair.

When she came to the door I said, 'Hello, would you like to see my baby and why have you got your dressing down on in the middle of the day?'

Mrs Winter said, 'Hello,' and smiled and all the cracks in her face changed shape. And then she said, 'It's not a dressing down, it's a dressing gown.'

Just like my Mum: It's not a dressing down it's a dressing gown, it's not Underground Road, it's Underdown Road and it's not an Australian terror but an Australian terrier. So I thought she must be a mother or a teacher.

'Yes, but why have you got it on?' I asked. 'And where are your children?'

She smiled again and said, 'I have it on because I want to.'

I liked the way she broke the rules like that; you're not supposed to wear your dressing down in the afternoon.

'And my children have grown up and moved away.'

I showed Mrs Winter (not Winter, Hinter) my baby Blackie and she bent down a little and said, 'What a beautiful baby. She has pretty eyes just like you.'

I looked down at Blackie's big, green shining eyes then back up at Mrs Winter's tiny eyes that were the colour of grey chalk and said, 'Goodbye.'

The second time I went to Mrs Winter's house, Mum and I saw her at the shop first. She had her dressing down on that day too. I could see it poking out from under her coat. She had pink slippers on and wore a black handbag over her arm.

'Hello,' I said and tugged her coat.

She looked down at me and put her hand to her chin but she didn't say anything. She turned around and shuffled away.

'Hello, Mrs Hinter,' Mum said. 'Are you all right?'

Mrs Winter just smiled her funny crackly smile and Mum said, 'Come on, I'll take you home.'

Mum led her gently out of the shop and down the street right to her house. We walked in through the gate and crunched our way over the gravel to the wide-open front door.

The house was dark inside because all the curtains were closed. Mum went in and opened them while Mrs Winter and I stood by the front door and waited. Then Mum took Mrs Winter's coat off, steered her into the kitchen and told her to sit while she made a cup of tea. Mrs Winter didn't say anything, she just sat down and folded her hands in her lap.

I had a look around Mrs Winter's little house. There were photographs in fancy frames and china ornaments of ladies and animals. They were all grey with dust. I ran my finger over the back of a horse and saw it was the colour of rust underneath.

A cat came and rubbed itself against my legs and purred and purred just like Blackie used to do. I picked her up and smelt her lovely warm cat smell. She was black like Blackie but her fur was shorter and silkier and her eyes were a glittery yellow not green like Blackie's. She wore a little red collar with a silver disk attached to it. The disk said T...E...S...S. So I knew her name was Tess.

'Look!' I carried Tess into the kitchen to show Mrs Winter how much her cat liked me.

Mrs Winter scratched Tess on the head and said, 'I had a black cat once.'

'This is your cat,' I said and held Tess a little closer to Mrs Winter in case her little eyes couldn't see properly.

She just looked at me and blinked.

'This is your cat,' I said again.

She put her hand up to her chin for a little while and then she smiled and said, 'You've found Sooty.'

I liked the way she changed the name of her cat. 'That's a nice name,' I told her. 'And it's imaginative.'

She smiled.

Then Mum asked me to go home. I put Sooty on Mrs Winter's lap and said goodbye.

I saw the tip of Mrs Winter's dressing down sleeve slip as her hand fell. The ambulance man lifted her arm carefully and put it under the sheet again. They put Mrs Winter into the back of the van and shut the doors.

'She couldn't have been murdered,' Rayleen told me, 'because there's no blood. There's always blood.'

We stood and watched the ambulance drive slowly down the road.

'No there isn't,' I said. And this time I knew, I really did know. 'You don't need blood for murder. There's strangling and choking and crushing and crunching.'

'And cracking,' Rayleen said with her hands on her hips. 'This time it was cracking.' She turned and skipped away. 'Come on. Let's do Pepper.'

But I knew she wasn't always right. Sometimes I was, here in Underground Road, where lots of things got murdered and not one had ever bled before.

Lucky Number 13

The small interview room is brightly lit by too many fluorescent lights and Edith feels exposed. She fidgets with the crumpled tissue in her hand and tries to calm her thudding heart.

'So where exactly did you say you lost your purse?' the social worker across the desk asks with her pen poised over a grey form.

'I'm not sure exactly,' Edith says. 'I think I left it on the bus when I was on my way to the shops but I may have left it at the bus stop.'

'And how much money was in it?'

'Oh about seventy dollars.'

The worker nods and says, 'I can see from your file that this has happened before.'

'Well…yes…but that was a while ago.'

'Actually, our records show that it was only three months ago.'

'Only three months,' Edith repeats, surprised.

'And the time before was about eleven months ago. So this will be the third time in a year that you've lost your purse.'

Edith doesn't know what to say. She feels light-headed. What if they won't help? What will she eat? She'll have to go to another food agency and do this all over again. She feels sick at the thought.

'Is there anything else we can help you with?'

'No, just a food voucher, thank you.'

'Is there anything you'd like to talk about?'

Edith looks at her blankly. 'About?'

'About losing money.'

She senses the conversation going in a dangerous direction.

'You've lost your purse three times this year. That's a lot of money to lose. '

'Yes, I guess it is,' Edith agrees, hoping this is the right answer, hoping the woman will let it go. The white plastic clock on the wall above the desk ticks loudly and she forces herself to breathe slowly while she waits for a reply or another question but there isn't one.

'I have been very forgetful lately,' Edith explains, finally. 'Perhaps I need to cut back on some medication or something.' She forces a smile and the worker seems reassured.

'Right then,' she says. 'I'll go and organise that voucher for you.'

Edith lets out a long quiet sigh when the woman leaves. She looks around the small room at the brightly coloured posters. Outside, the sky is a murky slate-grey. A hot flush creeps up her neck and she realises how overheated the room is. She picks up a pamphlet from the desk and fans herself for a moment to bring her temperature down. When she squints at the pamphlet, holds it at arms' length to read it, a lump instantly forms in her throat. 'Gamblers Anonymous… Gambling Counselling.' Was it left there for her? Could they know?

The door swings open and the woman strides in, sits down. Edith's body is still smarting from the shock of the pamphlet.

The worker's eyes flick to it but her expression gives nothing away. 'Here we are,' she says brightly, placing some paperwork on the desk. 'I just need a signature and you can be on your way.'

As Edith signs with a shaky hand, the worker says, 'I'm obligated to tell you that our policy only allows us to help with lost or stolen money once a year.' It is said slowly and carefully. 'We've made a couple of allowances for you but unfortunately this is the last time we can help in these circumstances.'

Shame prickles every pore on Edith's body. She does not look up, she folds the voucher and places it neatly into her handbag.

'Of course, if you have any other problems please don't hesitate to call. As you can see from all the brochures and posters in the room, there are many ways we can be of help.'

'Yes…thank you.' Edith hears her voice – a mousy little voice, a nothing little voice. She walks through the door into the chaos of the waiting area and then out into a strong wind and sleety rain toward the shopping centre. The interview belligerently replays in her mind…three times…our policy…lost and stolen money… If you have any other problems… They must know! The shame of it sends another searing prickle of heat over her body and she's glad to be out in the icy weather.

Her grey hair is plastered to her skull and her coat is drenched when the sliding glass doors of the shopping mall open. Inside, it is hot and busy despite the weather. People move in blurs around her. Edith feels surrounded by larger, sturdier people. She does not look at anyone directly. She could not imagine having a conversation right now. At the entrance of the supermarket she pulls out a trolley and wheels it into the store past a yellow plastic triangle that is repeating the words, 'Caution wet floor' in a robotic voice. Caution wet floor… our policy…lost and stolen money…

Edith sets her face in a scowl and wills herself to concentrate on food and on how she might best spend the voucher. She needs to make the most of it. She stands in the middle of the fruit and vegetable displays and stares at all the colour. What does she need? What can she afford? She takes a wedge of pumpkin and a bag of cheap carrots and places them in the bottom of the trolley. She inspects a branch of broccoli to gauge if it is fresh enough to last beyond the week.

A toddler in a trolley swings her legs back and forth and kicks the side of a nearby display stand. Thump, thump. Thump, thump.

'Stop it,' a mother warns.

Edith cowers. She feels like a small child herself. Feels as if she has been caught out at school for playing truant or worse, for stealing somebody's lunch. She has to stay away from those poker machines. She has to stay away from the club.

Thump, thump. Thump, thump.

'Stop it!' The mother raises her voice. 'Stop it now!'

Thump, thump! Thump, thump!

Edith wheels her trolley away from the noise and walks up and down the aisles stopping frequently to consider items. She can add up the total of a few things but the more she puts in the trolley, the more uneasy she feels. She hopes she has enough money to cover it all.

She picks up a bag of rice and one of pasta. She doesn't really like either but they are cheap and will last a long time. If she can make the food last longer, she might even be able to pay part of the electricity bill with next fortnight's pension. The red electricity bill sends another wave of despair through her. She tosses both packets into the trolley and moves on, trying not to think about overdue bills.

In the chilly air of the refrigerated section, she looks for cheese. She takes her time, making sure she has the cheapest block before placing it in her trolley. She spends the same time and consideration on mincemeat and ham and then heads toward the queues at the cash registers. She chooses the one on the end where there are fewest people. She hopes no one notices that she is paying with a food voucher. The line moves slowly. There's a book of puzzles in a nearby stand; she picks it up and flicks through to distract herself. She wonders if she'll have enough money left over to pay for it. It's only two dollars and it might give her something to do during the long afternoons. It might keep her away from the club.

The queue moves forward and Edith is next. She waits till there is space on the conveyor belt and then begins to load her shopping onto it.

'Chocate?'

'No.'

Edith recognises the voice of the kicking toddler's mother in the queue behind.

'Choc-ate!'

'Leave it!'

She glances at the mother and realises with horror that she lives in her street at Number 13. She looks at the shopping on the belt. She wants to put it back into her trolley, take off, find another queue, an anonymous queue. But she can't – it's too late; the operator has started to scan it.

'Skye! I said, leave it!'

Edith loads the rest of the shopping onto the belt and braces herself. She watches the total rise quickly as the blonde operator scans and packs the items. She feels herself plummet when the last item is checked through.

'That's fifty-three sevenny-five,' the operator says.

'Ah… I'll have to put something back,' Edith says quietly.

'What?' The operator frowns and turns her ear toward her.

'I don't have enough money.' Edith speaks a little louder.

The shop suddenly seems very quiet.

The operator raises an eyebrow. 'How much do you have?'

'Fifty dollars.' Edith fidgets in her bag for the voucher.

'What do you wanna put back?'

Where's the voucher? It's got to be in here.

'What do you want to put back?' the operator asks much louder.

Edith blinks. 'Um…the ham. Put the ham back.' The voucher is there, slipped neatly away. She hands it to the operator, who is sifting through the bags for the ham.

'It's a welfare cheque.'

Edith wishes she would speak quietly. She feels every eye behind burning holes in her back.

'You're supposed to go to the information desk with welfare cheques.'

She never had before. 'I –'

'Tell Leanne to come down to number twenny,' the operator says into her phone. 'I've got a welfare cheque.' She waves it in the air.

A dark-headed woman who looks vaguely familiar arrives; she takes the voucher and inspects it. 'No worries. I'll get the cash. Won't be a sec.' She touches Edith's arm and says softly, 'New system, love. Bring it to the information desk next time.'

The compassion, the pity is too much. There won't be a next time. There can't be a next time.

'You can't buy this with a welfare cheque.' The operator takes the crossword book out of one of the bags and holds it up.

How did that get through? She thought she'd put it back.

'You can only buy food.' The operator leans forward and says relatively quietly, 'You can't go spending taxpayers' money, my money, on just anything, you know.'

Edith feels as if she has been slapped. She grits her teeth and narrows her eyes. She would like to say that she was a taxpayer for over thirty years but she cannot speak.

The cash register blips as the book is rescanned and two dollars is deducted from the total.

'You're still one sevenny-five over.' The operator crosses her arms and stares.

The ham is worth about three dollars and Edith wonders if there is enough change in her purse to make up the deficit. She would like to keep the ham if she can. She opens her bag, pulls out her purse and looks inside at an assortment of five, ten and twenty cent pieces. She tips them into her palm.

The dark-haired woman returns with a fifty-dollar note. 'There you go,' she says to the operator before flitting away again.

Edith begins to count the coins in her hand but her mind won't focus. 'I have a little more money here,' she says passing it to the operator who counts it quickly.

'You're still fifty cents short.' She raises her eyebrows. 'Somethings gotta go back.'

Edith tries to remember what else she bought. What's the cheapest item? What can she do without? She feels the queue behind, breathing down her neck. She dithers. It's too much pressure. 'Forget the ham,' she says out of desperation.

'Here!' a familiar voice barks. 'Take this.' The mother from Number 13 leans over Edith, her fleshy fingers hold a fifty-cent piece.

The operator snatches the money.

Edith turns and looks into Number 13's face; she opens her mouth to say thank you but nothing comes out.

Number 13 smiles warmly at Edith. She cocks her head at the operator, leans in again and whispers, 'What a bitch.'